In memory of my grandfather, and for Chika Ekwensi

The publishers would like to thank James Morley of the Royal Botanic Gardens, Kew, England, and Dr H.M. Burkill, author of *The Useful Plants of Tropical West Africa* (Kew, England: Royal Botanic Gardens, 1995) for their help.

Published in the United States in 1998 by The Millbrook Press, Inc.
2 Old New Milford Road, Brookfield, Connecticut 06804

First published in Great Britain in 1998 by Frances Lincoln Limited,
4 Torriano Mews, Torriano Avenue, London NW5 2RZ

Text and illustrations © 1998 Ifeoma Onyefulu

Library of Congress Cataloging-in-Publication Data
Onyefulu, Ifeoma.
Grandfather's work : a traditional healer in Nigeria / by Ifeoma
Onyefulu.
p.   cm.
Includes bibliographical references.
Summary: A child describes the work of his grandfather, a
traditional healer in a Nigerian village, comparing it to the work
of other family members. Includes information about plants used in
healing.
ISBN 0-7613-0412-6 (lib. bdg.)
[1. Grandfathers--Fiction. 2. Healers--Fiction. 3. Nigeria-
-Fiction.]   I. Title.
PZ7.0575Gr 1998   97-35815
[E]--dc21   CIP
                                                        AC

The treatments described in this book require thorough knowledge and experience to prepare and administer. Many of the plants pictured or referred to resemble other plants whose physiological effects may be unpleasant or dangerous. Under no circumstances should any of the treatments described in this book be attempted.

Grandfather's Work

A Traditional Healer in Nigeria

IFEOMA ONYEFULU

THE MILLBROOK PRESS
BROOKFIELD, CONNECTICUT

Author's note

I am privileged to have had a grandfather, the late David Ekwensi, whose knowledge of plants, roots, tree-barks, and animals was vast. He usually spent six months of the year in the forest hunting, and his survival there was largely due to the powers of plants and roots. One day he was bitten by a snake; what saved his life were the plant juices he rubbed into the bite and the roots he boiled and drank.

I can remember my grandfather squeezing the juice out of a plant and giving it to my mother to drink when she had stomach cramps. As a child, watching him at work was pure magic, but as I grew older, I realized it was not magic—his healing power came from the plants he used.

At Nkwelle Ezuaka, his village in eastern Nigeria, my grandfather helped many sick people, and was well known as a healer. Often, people came back with gifts to thank him for curing them. He was made a chief in recognition of his contribution to the village.

All over the world, the healing properties of plants, roots, and tree-barks form the basis of traditional medicine. People use dock leaves to relieve nettle-sting, while aloe vera leaves bring relief to sunburned skin. However, the use of all plants, roots, and tree-barks requires expert knowledge.

Healing power tends to run in families, and valuable knowledge is passed down from generation to generation—although many people have now rejected traditional healing in favor of modern Western medicines.

I have written this book to keep alive the memory of my grandfather.

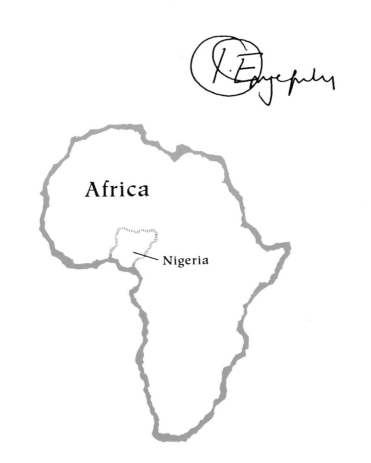

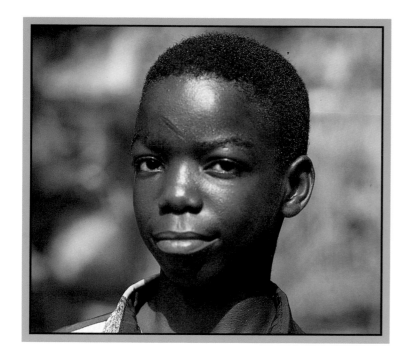 

My grandfather is a magician. He uses leaves, roots, and bark from trees and plants to help people who are ill or need help. Anyone with a problem can go to him for advice. People often say thank you by giving him a goat or a chicken.

He is very special. Last year, when there was a big festival in my village, he stood up like a great tree and made a speech wishing the people well. The clapping that greeted him sounded like thunder.

His work is different from everyone else's in my family. And we're a big family. Let me tell you about some of them.

My grandmother makes wedding gowns, party dresses, and clothes for special occasions. She says it takes about two weeks to make a chief's robes, because she has to find special threads and buttons.

When she looks at the clothes she has made, her heart is filled with happiness.

My father teaches grown-ups in a big school. Later on, these grown-ups will teach children.

Here is my father at work. He is very clever. Grandfather is very clever and his work makes him happy, too, but his work is different from my grandmother's and my father's.

My mother owns a bakery. Here she is buying flour and salt for baking bread. She has five bakers to make and bake the bread.

Her bread is delicious! People come in every day to buy it.

Here are my mother and two of her bakers, packing loaves
into bags.

My mother works hard at home, too. I think she has magic
powers. But they are very different from Grandfather's magic powers.

My uncle carves things out of wood. Great-grandfather taught him how to make wooden masks, dolls, and animals when he was a little boy. People often send my uncle photographs of things they want him to make. Today he is carving antelopes.

My uncle can make almost anything out of wood. Last week he carved a door for the chief of our village, and this is what it looked like.

He loves his work. Grandfather loves his work, too, but his work is very different from my uncle's.

Uncle Law (that's what everyone calls him) has to wear these funny-looking clothes when he goes to work at a place called the High Court. I think the clothes make him look like a giant.

When someone is in trouble, Uncle Law stands up and speaks for them in Court. He really cares about people.

This is my favorite auntie, who makes pots. She collects clay from the river bank in our village. Then she starts to mold a small lump of clay, turning it around and adding more and more clay as she forms the shape.

Here she is taking dry pots out of the fire. My auntie knows a lot about earth and clay. Grandfather knows a lot and he really cares about people, too, but his work is different from Uncle Law's and my auntie's.

My favorite uncle makes
things out of iron. He melts
the iron in the fire and
before it cools, he quickly
beats it into the shape he
wants with a heavy hammer.
He makes knives, keys, and
other things, too.
Here he is pumping his
bellows to make a fire.

And here he is holding a hoe he made. My uncle says it can be hard work, and that is why young people do not want to do this kind of work anymore. One day, there will be no more blacksmiths in our family.

My uncle is strong. Grandfather is strong, too, but his work is different from my favorite uncle's.

Auntie Ngo is a doctor. She knows about all kinds of illness because she studied them for seven years. Now she helps people, especially women, get better. Grandfather helps people get better, too, but his work is different even from Auntie Ngo's.

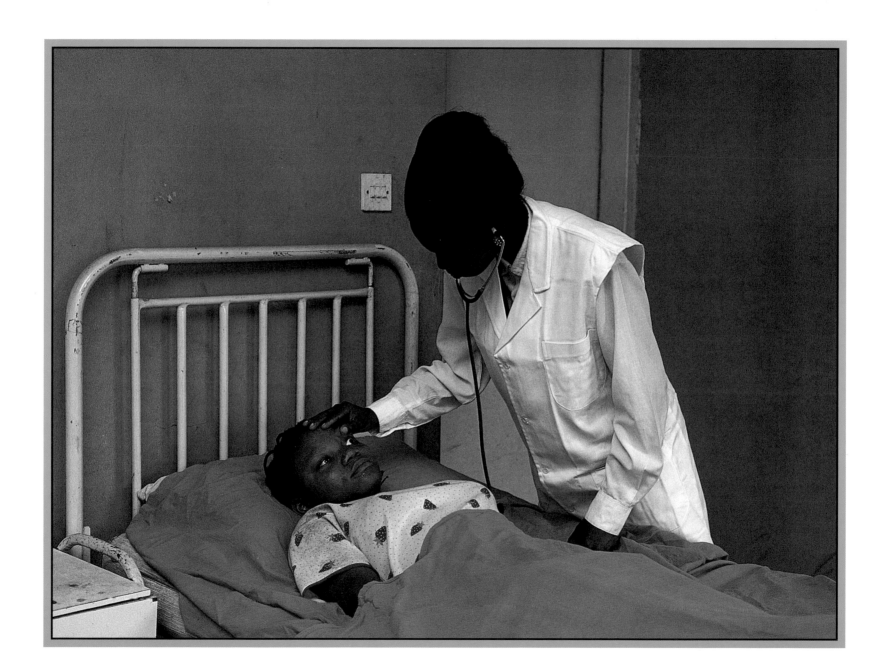

Yesterday I went to see Grandfather. He was healing a patient's leg. He used leaves to clean it, then rubbed in a herb mixture.

Afterward, I said to him, "Grandfather, you are a magician. I know you are."

He smiled, "What makes you say that, child?"

"You know a lot about plants. And you walk many miles into the forest to collect them. That is magic!"

He shook his head.

"No, child." He picked up his staff. "Look—this staff is special. It shows I am only a messenger. I carry healing messages to sick people.

"When I was small like you, my grandmother took me into the forest and taught me about the powers of plants and trees. She told me to pick only what I needed, and not to waste anything. Plants and trees are very important to us, to the animals, and to the whole world. Sometimes we forget how special they are."

"Now," Grandfather said, "I want you to use your ears, eyes, and nose, because I am going to show you some of the powers of plants and trees. But remember, you must not use any of these, because you are still a child. I waited until I was 35 years old and had learned a lot more about healing before I started to use them on patients."

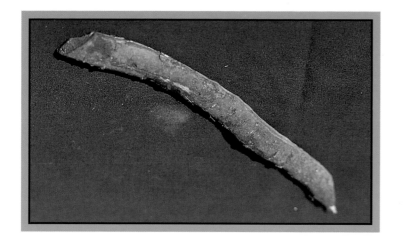

He pointed to a root.

"We call this *okpokolo*. When the root is boiled in water and the juice is drunk, it brings down a fever.

"*Osencha* is what we call this root. We boil it and use the juice to treat chest and hip pains.

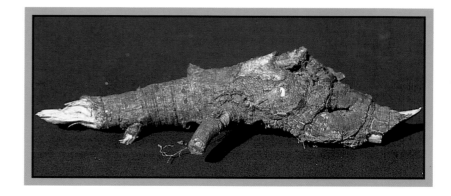

"We call this plant *nsi ebilibi*. We squeeze the juice from the leaves, mix it with a little water, and give it as a drink to stop stomach pains."

Then Grandfather pointed to a small tree.

"This is called *dogoyaro*. This one is still a young tree, but it will grow much bigger. We squeeze the leaves into a little water and use the liquid to treat malaria, which is caused by mosquito bites. If I give a sick person dogoyaro juice to drink several times a day, the fever usually flies away.

"But if it doesn't go, I give them a steaming pot of dogoyaro leaves and roots to inhale. I put layers of cloth on top of them to make them sweat quickly, and leave them alone for about five minutes. Then I strain the liquid from the pot into a bowl of cold water for them to wash in."

Grandfather looked at me with sad eyes. "But no one wants to drink dogoyaro anymore."

"Why not, Grandfather?" I asked.

"Everything is changing. No one likes to drink medicine unless it is sweet. And only a few people want to go into the forest or climb trees to collect these precious roots and leaves. We want everything to happen very quickly nowadays. It breaks my heart."

"But Grandfather," I said, "I want to be like you, and know all the powers of plants and trees."

He smiled. "And do you really want to visit the forest to see where they grow?" he asked.

"Yes, Grandfather, I do."

He smiled again.

"My child, you have made an old man very happy. But you will have to study hard before you know what I know. Many plants look alike—and while some can be used as medicine, others are harmful.

"Now I must go. I have to collect plants before nightfall—but we'll start tomorrow."

My eyes followed my grandfather as he walked swiftly up the road holding his big knife. He got smaller and smaller until he vanished out of sight.

Now my heart is beating very fast, because I can't wait to be walking up that road with my grandfather tomorrow.

A note about Grandfather's plants

Not long ago, little attention would have been paid to Grandfather's extraordinary knowledge of local plants; indeed, people may even have regarded him as a witch doctor. But in recent years, scientists looking for new ways to treat illnesses have begun to discover that many traditional folk medicines really work. Now, ethnobotany—the science of plants, people, and culture—is very important, with scientists all over the world working together to gather information and analyze plant extracts, before many rare and valuable plants on our planet become extinct.

Two of Grandfather's plants have been identified by ethnobotanists:

Dogoyaro *(Azadirachta indica, Family: Meliaceae) has recently been shown to contain effective antimalarial compounds. In Asia, it is known as neem.*

Okpokolo *(Anthocleista djalensis, Family: Loganiaceae) is a plant whose parts are reported to be active pharmacologically, especially the root. It has been used in traditional West African medicine to treat many conditions.*

It has not yet been possible to identify **osencha** *and* **nsi ebilibi**. *All the plants and roots in this book were photographed in the local government area of Anambra, in southeastern Nigeria, and their names are given in Ntiange, one of the many dialects spoken by the Igbo tribe.*